TO KIM
ON HIS 7th BIRTHDAY ♥
with lots of love
from Mummy & Daddy

NURSERY
PETER PAN

'*The Nursery Peter Pan* is a book
that will surely be widely
welcomed by all who have
charge of little children of three
or four and upwards . . . The
editing has been done with a
keen sensitivity — nothing is
spoiled or altered . . . real
little-children illustrations, safe,
warm and comforting,
even when they are full of pirates.'

GOOD HOUSEKEEPING

J. M. BARRIE

EDITED BY OLIVE JONES

THE NURSERY
PETER PAN

ILLUSTRATED BY

MABEL LUCIE ATTWELL

AND J. S. GOODALL

HODDER AND STOUGHTON

LONDON SYDNEY AUCKLAND TORONTO

Do you know that this book is part of the J. M. Barrie
'Peter Pan Bequest'?
This means that J. M. Barrie's royalty on this book goes
to help the doctors and nurses to cure the children who
are lying ill in Great Ormond Street Hospital, London

ISBN O 340 03703 2

This edition copyright © 1961 Hodder and Stoughton Ltd
Eleventh impression 1981

Printed Offset Litho and bound in Great Britain for
Hodder and Stoughton Children's Books,
a division of Hodder and Stoughton Ltd,
Mill Road, Dunton Green, Sevenoaks, Kent TN13 2YJ, by
Fakenham Press Ltd, Fakenham, Norfolk

Contents

1 - Peter Breaks Through

ALL children, except one, grow up. This is the story of that one – Peter Pan. . . .

Mr and Mrs Darling lived at Number 14 with their three children, Wendy, John and Michael. Their nurse was a Newfoundland dog called Nana. There never was a simpler, happier family until the coming of Peter Pan.

He came from a make-believe island called the Neverland. It was an island in the children's minds, where they used to play happily.

Wendy told her mother that Peter Pan sat at the foot of the bed and played music on his pipes to her. Mrs Darling said she must have been dreaming. Then one evening she saw him with her own eyes.

It was Nana's evening out, and Mrs Darling sat by the nursery fire with her sewing. Soon she fell asleep. The window blew open, and a boy dropped on the floor. With him was a strange light which darted about the room.

Mrs Darling knew at once that the boy must be Peter Pan. She screamed, and at that moment Nana rushed in. She growled and sprang at the boy, who leapt lightly through the window. Poor Mrs Darling thought he must be killed, for the window was three floors up. She ran down into the street to look for his body, but it was not there. She only saw what she thought was a shooting star in the black night sky.

When she went back to the nursery she found Nana with the boy's shadow in her mouth. As he had leapt at the window Nana had closed it quickly and snapped the shadow off. Mrs Darling rolled it up and put it carefully in a drawer.

On Friday night, just a week later, Mr and Mrs Darling were getting ready to go out to dinner at Number 27 when Nana came in with Michael's bottle of medicine in her mouth. But he was naughty and refused to take it.

'Won't, won't,' he cried.

Mr Darling said he must be brave, and he offered to take a spoonful of *his* medicine, which was much nastier. But he only pretended to take it, and poured it into Nana's bowl. It looked like milk, and Nana began to lap it up. She knew at once that he had played a trick on her, and she gave him a sad look and crept into her kennel in the nursery.

The children were very upset. Mr Darling was ashamed of himself and furious with Nana.

'The proper place for you is the yard,' he said. He dragged Nana out, and tied her up in the backyard.

So there was no Nana in the nursery that night to take care of the children after Mr and Mrs Darling had gone out.

Almost as soon as they had gone the three night-lights in the nursery flickered and went out. There was another light in the room, a thousand times brighter. When it came to rest for a second you saw it was a fairy: Tinker Bell. She flashed about the room, looking for Peter's shadow.

A moment later Peter Pan followed her through the window. He had carried Tinker Bell part of the way, and his hand was still messy with fairy dust.

'Tinker Bell,' he called softly. 'Where are you?'

A tinkle as of golden bells answered him. It was the fairy language, which children cannot understand. Tinker Bell told Peter that his shadow was in the chest of drawers. Peter jumped at it and pulled

9

out his shadow – but he shut Tinker Bell in a drawer by mistake.

Then he tried to stick his shadow on. It wouldn't stick. He tried again with soap from the bathroom, but that also failed. Peter sat on the floor and cried. His sobs woke Wendy and she sat up in bed.

'What's your name?' he asked.

'Wendy Moira Angela Darling,' she replied, and asked him where he lived.

'Second to the right,' said Peter, 'and then straight on till morning.'

'What a funny address!' said Wendy.

'No, it isn't,' said Peter.

'I mean,' said Wendy politely, 'is that what they put on the letters?'

'Don't get any letters,' said Peter.

'But your mother gets letters?'

'Don't have a mother,' he said, and Wendy was very sorry for him.

'Oh, Peter, no wonder you were crying,' she said.

'I wasn't crying about mothers,' said Peter. 'I was crying because I can't get my shadow to stick on. Besides, I wasn't crying.'

Wendy saw the shadow on the floor. Fortunately she knew at once what to do.

'It must be sewn on,' she said, and began to sew

the shadow to his foot. It hurt a little, but soon his shadow was sewn on and behaving properly.

Peter jumped about in glee, quite forgetting what Wendy had done for him. He thought he had sewn on the shadow himself.

'How clever I am,' he crowed. In fact there never was a cockier boy than Peter. Wendy was cross with him. He said he was sorry, but he couldn't help crowing when he was pleased with himself. 'Wendy,'

he said, 'Wendy, one girl is more use than twenty boys.'

'Do you really think so, Peter?' asked Wendy.

'Yes, I do.'

She said she would give him a kiss if he liked. But Peter did not know what a kiss was, and held out his hand for it.

'Surely you know what a kiss is?' she asked.

'I shall know when you give it to me,' he replied stiffly; and not to hurt his feelings she gave him a thimble.

Then Peter said he would give *her* a kiss, but he merely dropped an acorn button into her hand. Wendy said she would wear his kiss on the chain round her neck. It was lucky that she did put it on that chain, for it was afterwards to save her life.

Wendy asked Peter how old he was.

'I don't know,' he replied uneasily, 'but I am quite young. I ran away the day I was born. It was because I heard father and mother talking about what I was to be when I became a man. I don't want ever to be a man. I want always to be a little boy and have fun. So I ran away to Kensington Gardens and lived among the fairies.'

He told Wendy about the beginning of fairies.

'You see, Wendy, when the first baby laughed for the first time, its laugh broke into a thousand pieces, and that was the beginning of fairies. But children know such a lot now, they soon don't believe in fairies, and every time a child says, "I don't believe in fairies", a fairy somewhere falls down dead.'

It struck him that Tinker Bell was keeping very quiet. 'I can't think where she has gone to,' he said. 'She was here just now. You don't hear her, do you?' and they both listened.

'The only sound I hear,' said Wendy, 'is like a tinkle of bells.'

The sound came from the chest of drawers, and Peter made a merry face. 'Wendy,' he whispered gleefully, 'I do believe I shut her up in the drawer!'

He let poor Tink out of the drawer, and she flew about the nursery screaming with fury. She spoke in fairy language, so that Wendy could not understand what she said.

'Oh, Peter,' Wendy cried, 'if only she would stand still and let me see her!'

At that moment Tinker Bell came to rest on the cuckoo clock. 'Oh the lovely!' cried Wendy. 'But what does she say, Peter?'

He had to translate. 'She is not very polite. She says you are a great ugly girl.'

Peter and Wendy were sitting together in the armchair, and he told her that he lived with the lost boys – 'children who fall out of their perambulators when the nurse is looking the other way. If they are not claimed in seven days they are sent far away to the Neverland. I'm their captain.'

'What fun it must be!' said Wendy.

'Yes,' said cunning Peter, 'but we are rather lonely. You see we have no female companionship. Girls, you know, are much too clever to fall out of their prams.'

'I think,' said Wendy, 'it is perfectly lovely the way you talk about girls. John there just despises us.'

For reply Peter rose and kicked John out of bed, blankets and all: one kick. Wendy was angry, but John went on sleeping so placidly on the floor that she let him stay there.

'I know you meant to be kind,' she said to Peter, 'so you may give me a kiss.'

For the moment she had forgotten his ignorance about kisses. 'I thought you would want it back,' he said a little bitterly, and offered to return her the thimble.

'Oh dear,' said Wendy. 'I don't mean a kiss, I mean a thimble.'

'What's that?'

'It's like this.' She kissed him.

'Funny!' said Peter. 'Now shall I give you a thimble?'

'If you wish to,' said Wendy. Peter thimbled her, and almost immediately she screeched. She told Peter it was exactly as if someone had pulled her hair.

'That must have been Tink,' said Peter. 'I never knew her so naughty before.'

She was disappointed when Peter said that he had come to the nursery window not to see her but to listen to stories.

'You see,' he said, 'none of the lost boys know any stories. Do you know why swallows build in the eaves of houses? It is to listen to the stories. Oh Wendy, your mother was telling you such a lovely story – about the prince who couldn't find the lady who wore the glass slipper.'

'That was Cinderella,' said Wendy.

Peter began to draw her towards the window, begging her to go with him and tell stories to the

15

other boys. 'I'll teach you to fly,' he said. 'And Wendy, there are mermaids, with such long tails. And you could tuck us in at night – and darn our clothes and make pockets for us. None of us has any pockets.'

She ran to John and Michael and shook them. 'Wake up,' she cried. 'Peter Pan has come and he is to teach us to fly.'

John rubbed his eyes. 'Then I shall get up,' he said. Then he saw that he was on the floor already. 'Hallo,' he said, 'I *am* up!'

Michael was up too. Peter suddenly signed silence. Nana, who had been barking in distress all the evening, was quiet now. She knew that something was wrong in the nursery.

'Out with the light! Hide! Quick!' cried John. When Liza, Mrs Darling's little maid, came in with Nana, the nursery was dark. The children were hiding behind the window curtains.

Liza was in a bad temper, for she was mixing the Christmas puddings in the kitchen, and had been drawn away from them by Nana's absurd suspicions. She thought the best way of getting a little quiet was to take Nana to the nursery – but on a lead.

'There, see for yourself,' she said. 'The children are perfectly safe, sound asleep in bed. Listen to their gentle breathing.'

Here Michael breathed so loudly that they were nearly detected. Nana knew that kind of breathing, and she tried to get free. But Liza pulled her out of the room. She tied the unhappy dog up again, and went back to her puddings.

But Nana strained and strained at her chain until at last she broke it. In another moment she had burst into the dining-room at Number 27 and flung up her paws to show something was wrong. Mr and Mrs Darling knew at once that something terrible was happening in their nursery, and they rushed into the street.

But ten minutes had passed, and Peter Pan can do a great deal in ten minutes.

In the nursery the children emerged from behind the curtains, and John asked, 'I say, Peter, can you really fly?'

Instead of troubling to answer him, Peter flew round the room. It looked very easy and they tried it, but they always went down instead of up.

Peter showed them again, both slowly and quickly. But no one can fly unless the fairy dust has been blown on him. Fortunately one of Peter's hands was messy with it, and he blew some on each of them, with the most superb results.

'Now just wriggle your shoulders this way,' he said, 'and let go.'

They were all on their beds. Michael let go first. At once he was borne across the room. 'I flewed!' he screamed, while still in mid-air.

John let go and met Wendy near the bathroom. 'Look at me!'

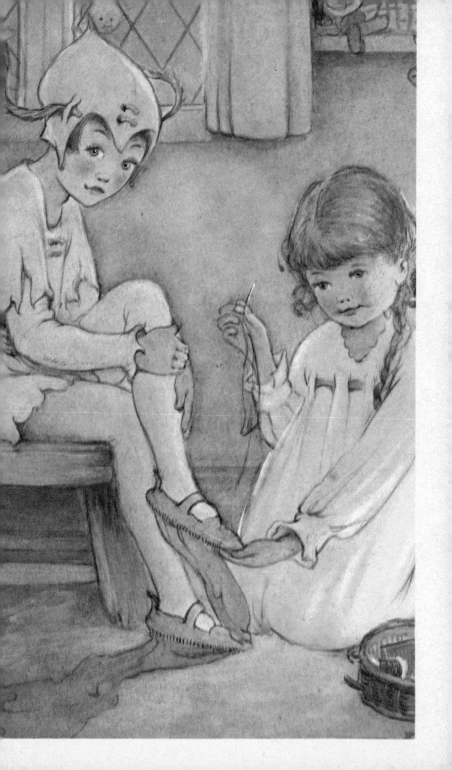

Up and down they went, and round and round. 'I say,' cried John. 'Why shouldn't we all go out?'

Of course Peter had been luring them to this all the time, but Wendy hesitated.

'Mermaids!' said Peter again. 'And there are pirates.'

'Pirates,' cried John, seizing his Sunday hat. 'Let's go at once.'

It was just at this moment that Mr and Mrs Darling hurried with Nana out of Number 27. They ran into the middle of the street to look up at the nursery window. The room was ablaze with light, and they could see in shadow on the curtain three little figures in night attire circling round and round in the air. Not three figures – four!

Mr and Mrs Darling and Nana rushed into the nursery too late. The birds were flown.

2 - The Flight

'SECOND to the right, and straight on till morning.' That, Peter told Wendy, was the way to the Neverland. John and Michael raced each other in the air, and they would all go chasing each other gaily for miles.

They were sleepy, and that was a danger, for the moment they dropped off, down they fell.

'Save him! Save him!' Wendy would cry, as Michael suddenly dropped like a stone. Peter would dive down and catch him just before he could strike the sea; but he always waited till the last moment.

So at last they drew near the Neverland. 'There it is,' said Peter calmly.

Wendy and John and Michael stood on tiptoe in the air to get their first sight of the island. They all recognized it at once, because they had so often pretended to be there. They cried out that they could see the flamingo with a broken leg, Michael's cave, and in the brushwood nearby a wolf with her babies.

Peter was a little annoyed with them for knowing so much, but his triumph was at hand, for fear fell upon them. It came as the sun went down, leaving the island in gloom. And now the Neverland which had been make-believe when they had been at home was real, and it was getting darker every moment.

They were flying low. They could see nothing horrid, but they were finding it hard to fly. It was as if they had to push the air. Sometimes they hung in it until Peter had beaten on it with his fists.

'They don't want us to land,' he explained.

'Who are they?' Wendy whispered, shuddering, but he could not or would not say.

John asked if there were many pirates on the island just now, and Peter said he had never known so many. 'Hook is their captain,' he said, and Michael began to cry, for the children had heard how wicked Hook was.

Peter told them how he had cut off Hook's hand in a fight, so that now he had an iron hook instead of a right hand.

All this time Tinker Bell was flying with them making a circle of light round them. Wendy quite liked this, until Peter pointed out the drawbacks. The pirates had sighted them before the darkness came, and got out Long Tom, their big gun. If they saw Tink's light, they might fire at it. Tink's light

22

only went out when she was asleep. So they decided that she should travel in John's hat, which Wendy carried.

They flew on in silence; but suddenly the air was rent by a most tremendous crash. The pirates had fired Long Tom.

The roar of it echoed through the mountains. John and Michael found themselves alone in the darkness. Peter had been carried by the wind of the shot far out to sea, while Wendy was blown upwards with no companion but Tinker Bell.

Tinker Bell at once began to lure Wendy to her

destruction. Tink was not all bad; or rather, she was all bad just now, but sometimes she was all good. Fairies have to be one thing or the other, because being so small they unfortunately have room for one feeling only at a time. At present she was bad because she was full of jealousy of Wendy. What she said in her lovely tinkle sounded kind to Wendy, but it wasn't really. Tink flew back and forwards, plainly meaning, 'Follow me, and all will be well.'

What else could poor Wendy do? She did not know that Tink hated her. And so, staggering in her flight, she followed Tink to her doom.

3 - The Island Come True

IN Peter's absence things are usually quiet on the island of Neverland. The fairies take an hour longer in the morning, the beasts attend to their young, the redskins feed heavily for six days and nights, and when pirates and lost boys meet they merely bite their thumbs at each other. But with the coming of Peter they are all under way again.

There were six boys on the island, counting the Twins as two.

Tootles was very sweet-natured, and the humblest of the boys. Nibs was a gay boy. Slightly cut whistles out of the trees, and danced to his own tunes. He was the most conceited of the boys.

Curly was always up to mischief. Last came the Twins, who were exactly alike.

The pirates were on the track of the boys, singing their dreadful song:

> *'Avast belay, yo ho, heave to,*
> *A-pirating we go,*
> *And if we're parted by a shot,*
> *We're sure to meet below!'*

There never was a more villainous lot: handsome Cecco, with pieces of eight in his ears as ornaments; Jukes, every inch of him tattooed; the Irish bo'sun, Smee, an oddly genial man who stabbed, so to speak, without offence; and many other ruffians.

The blackest of them all was James Hook, or, as he wrote himself, Jas Hook. Instead of a right hand he had an iron hook. He was gaunt and dark, and his hair was dressed in long curls which looked like black candles. His eyes were of the blue of the forget-me-not, and melancholy, save when he was plunging his hook into you, at which time two red spots appeared in them and lit them up horribly. He was polite, and his speech was elegant. A man of courage, the only thing he was afraid of was the sight of his own blood, which was thick and of an unusual colour.

On the trail of the pirates came the redskins. They

carried tomahawks and knives, and their naked bodies gleamed with paint and oil. Strung around them were scalps. Bringing up the rear, the place of greatest danger, came Tiger Lily, a princess. She was very beautiful, and the belle of the Piccaninnies.

The redskins were followed by the beasts: lions,

tigers, bears, and many smaller things that flee from them. Last came a gigantic crocodile, looking for someone.

The boys, the pirates, the redskins and the beasts were all following one another round the island. Soon the boys appeared again. They flung themselves down on the grass, close to their underground home.

'I do wish Peter would come back,' they said, 'and tell us whether he has heard anything more about Cinderella.'

While they talked they heard a distant sound. It was the grim song:

> *'Yo ho, yo ho, the pirate life,*
> *The flag o' skull and bones,*
> *A merry hour, a hempen rope,*
> *And hey for Davy Jones.'*

Nibs darted away to spy on the pirates, but the boys went to their home under the ground. There

was no entrance to it to be seen, but there were seven large trees, each having in its hollow trunk a hole as large as a boy. They were the seven entrances to the home under the ground, for which Hook had been searching these many moons.

As the pirates advanced, Starkey sighted Nibs in the wood, and at once his pistol flashed out. But an iron claw gripped his shoulder.

'Put back that pistol!' said the black voice of Hook.

'It was one of those boys you hate,' said Starkey. 'I could have shot him dead.'

'Aye, and the sound would have brought Tiger Lily's redskins upon us. Do you want to lose your scalp?'

'Shall I after him, captain,' asked Smee, 'and tickle him with Johnny Corkscrew?' That was what Smee called his cutlass.

'Not now, Smee,' Hook said darkly. 'I want to catch all the seven. Scatter and look for them.'

The pirates disappeared among the trees, but Smee stayed with Captain Hook, who said that most of all he wanted to catch Peter Pan. ' 'Twas he cut off my arm. He flung it,' he said, wincing, 'to a crocodile that happened to be passing by. It liked my arm so much, Smee, that it has followed me ever since, licking its lips for the rest of me.'

MABEL
LUCIE
ATTWELL

He sat down on a large mushroom. 'Smee,' he said huskily, 'that crocodile would have had me before this, but by a lucky chance it swallowed a clock which goes *tick, tick, tick* inside it, and so before it can reach me I hear the tick and bolt.

'Some day,' said Smee, 'the clock will run down, and then he'll get you.'

Hook wetted his dry lips. 'Aye,' he said, 'that's the fear that haunts me. Smee,' he cried suddenly, 'this seat is hot.' He jumped up. 'Odds bobs, hammer and tongs, I'm burning.'

The big mushroom came away in their hands, for it had no root. Smoke began at once to ascend. They looked at each other. 'A chimney!' they both exclaimed.

They had indeed discovered the chimney of the home under the ground. Not only smoke came out of it. There came also boys' voices, for they were gaily chattering. The pirates listened grimly, and then replaced the mushroom. They looked around them, and noted the holes in the seven trees.

'Did you hear them say Peter Pan's away from home?' Smee whispered. Hook nodded. A curdling smile lit up his swarthy face.

'Unrip your plan, captain,' Smee cried eagerly.

'To return to the ship,' Hook replied, 'and cook a large rich cake of a jolly thickness with green sugar

on it. There can be but one room below, for there
is but one chimney. The silly moles had not the sense
to see that they did not need a door apiece. That
shows they have no mother. We will leave the cake
on the shore of the mermaids' lagoon. The boys will
find the cake and gobble it up, because, having no
mother, they don't know how dangerous 'tis to eat
rich damp cake.' He burst into laughter. 'Aha, they
will die.'

Hook and Smee danced and sang, but a sound
broke in; at first tiny, but as it came nearer it was
more distinct: *tick, tick, tick, tick*. Hook stood
shuddering, one foot in the air.

'The crocodile,' he gasped, and bounded away, followed by his bo'sun. It was indeed the crocodile. It oozed on after Hook.

Once more the boys emerged into the open; but the dangers of the night were not yet over, for presently Nibs rushed into their midst, pursued by a pack of wolves.

'Save me, save me!' cried Nibs, falling on the ground.

'But what can we do?' cried the boys, and almost in the same breath they added, 'Peter would look at them through his legs. Let us do what Peter would do.'

It is quite the most successful way of defying wolves, and as one boy they bent and looked through their legs. The wolves dropped their tails and fled.

Now Nibs rose from the ground. 'I have seen a wonderfuller thing,' he cried. 'A great white bird. It is flying this way. It looks so weary, and as it flies it moans, "Poor Wendy".'

'See, it comes,' cried Curly, pointing to Wendy in the heavens. She was now almost overhead, and they could hear her plaintive cry. But more distinct came the shrill voice of Tinker Bell. The jealous fairy was darting at her victim from every direction, pinching savagely every time she touched.

'Hallo, Tink,' cried the wondering boys.

Tink's reply rang out: 'Peter wants you to shoot the Wendy.'

Tootles had a bow and arrow with him, and Tink noted it, and rubbed her little hands. 'Quick, Tootles, quick,' she screamed. 'Peter will be so pleased.'

Tootles fitted the arrow to his bow. Then he fired, and Wendy fluttered to the ground with an arrow in her breast.

4 - The Little House

FOOLISH Tootles stood like a conqueror over Wendy's body. 'I have shot the Wendy,' he cried proudly. 'Peter will be so pleased with me.'

The others crowded round Wendy, and a terrible silence fell upon the wood. Slightly was the first to speak. 'This is no bird,' he said in a scared voice. 'I think it must be a lady.'

'And we have killed her,' Nibs said hoarsely. They all whipped off their caps.

'A lady to take care of us at last,' said one of the Twins, 'and you have killed her.'

Tootles' face was very white. 'I did it,' he said. 'I shot her.'

It was at this tragic moment that they heard Peter crow. 'Hide her,' they whispered, and gathered hastily around Wendy. But Tootles stood aloof.

Again came that ringing crow, and Peter dropped in front of them. 'Greetings, boys,' he cried. 'Great news. I have brought at last a mother for you all.'

There was no sound, except a little thud as Tootles dropped on his knees.

'Have you not seen her?' asked Peter, becoming troubled. 'She flew this way.'

Tootles rose. 'Peter,' he said quietly, 'I will show her to you;' and when the others would still have hidden her he said, 'Back, Twins, let Peter see.'

So they all stood back, and let him see.

'She is dead,' Peter said. He took the arrow from her heart and faced his band. 'Whose arrow?' he demanded sternly.

'Mine, Peter,' said Tootles on his knees; and Peter would have killed him with it but at that moment Wendy raised her arm.

Nibs bent over her and listened. 'I think she said, "Poor Tootles",' he whispered.

'She lives,' Peter said briefly. Then he knelt beside her and found his button on a chain round her neck. 'See,' he said, 'the arrow struck against this. It is the kiss I gave her. It has saved her life.'

Then they had to tell Peter of Tink's crime, and almost never had they seen him look so stern. 'Listen,

Tinker Bell,' he cried; 'I am your friend no more. Begone from me for ever.'

She flew on his shoulder and pleaded; but not until Wendy again raised her arm did he relent and say, 'Well, not for ever, but for a whole week.'

'Let us carry Wendy down into the house,' Curly suggested.

'No, no,' Peter said. 'Let us build a little house round her.'

They were all delighted. 'Quick,' he ordered them, 'bring me each of you the best of what we have. Gut our house. Be sharp.'

The boys scurried this way and that – down for bedding, up for firewood, and while they were at it, who should appear but John and Michael. They were very relieved to find Peter. He was very busy measuring Wendy with his feet to see how large a house she would need. Of course he meant to leave room for chairs and a table. John and Michael watched him.

'Curly,' said Peter, in his most captainy voice, 'see that those boys help in the building of the house.'

John and Michael were dragged away to hack and hew and carry. 'Chairs and a fender first,' Peter ordered. 'Then we shall build the house round them.'

Peter thought of everything. The wood was alive with the sound of axes.

'If only we knew,' said one, 'the kind of house she likes best.'

Without opening her eyes, Wendy began to sing:

> *'I wish I had a little house*
> *The littlest ever seen,*
> *With funny little red walls*
> *And roof of mossy green.'*

By the greatest good luck the branches they had brought were sticky with red sap, and the ground was carpeted with moss. When they had finished the cottage they made-believe to grow the loveliest roses up the walls.

'There's no chimney,' Peter said. 'We must have a chimney.' He snatched the hat off John's head, knocked out the bottom, and put the hat on the roof. Smoke immediately began to come out of it. Now really and truly it was finished.

The door opened and Wendy came out. 'Lovely, darling house,' she said.

Then they all went on their knees, and cried, 'O Wendy lady, be our mother.'

'Ought I?' Wendy said. 'I am only a little girl.'

'That doesn't matter,' said Peter. 'What we need is just a nice motherly person.'

'Very well,' she said. 'I will do my best. Come inside at once, you naughty children; I am sure your feet are damp. And before I put you to bed I have just time to finish the story of Cinderella.'

In they went. I don't know how there was room for them, but you can squeeze very tight in the Neverland. And that was the first of many joyous evenings they had with Wendy, pretending that she was their mother and Peter was their father.

By and by she tucked the boys up in the great bed in the home under the ground; but she herself slept that night in the little house, and Peter kept watch outside with drawn sword, for the pirates could be

heard carousing far away and the wolves were on the prowl. After a time he fell asleep, and some fairies had to climb over him on their way home. They tweaked his nose and passed on.

One of the first things Peter did next day was to measure Wendy and John and Michael for hollow trees. Hook had sneered at the boys for thinking they needed a tree apiece, but this was ignorance, for unless your tree fitted you it was difficult to go up and down, and no two of the boys were quite the same size. Once you fitted, you drew in your breath at the top, and down you went at exactly the right

MABEL
LUCIE
ATTWELL

speed; while to ascend you drew in and let out alternately, and so wriggled up.

But you simply must fit. After a few days' practice Wendy and John and Michael could go up and down as gaily as buckets in a well. And how ardently they grew to love their home under the ground; especially Wendy.

It consisted of one large room, with a floor in which grew stout mushrooms which were used as stools. A Never tree tried hard to grow in the centre of the room, but every morning they sawed the trunk through, level with the floor. By tea-time it was always about two feet high, and then they put a door on top of it to make a table.

The bed was tilted against the wall by day, and let down at 6.30, when it filled nearly half the room; and all the boys except Michael slept in it, lying like sardines in a tin. There was a strict rule against turning round until one gave the signal, when they all turned at once. Michael should have used it also; but Wendy would have a baby, and he was the littlest, so he was put in a basket.

There was one recess in the wall, no larger than a bird-cage, which was the private apartment of Tinker Bell. It could be shut off from the rest of the home by a tiny curtain.

It was all especially entrancing to Wendy because

those rampageous boys of hers gave her so much to
do. The cooking kept her nose to the pot. Their
chief food was roasted bread-fruit, yams, coconuts,
baked pig, mammee-apples, tappa rolls and
bananas, washed down with calabashes of poe-poe;
but you never exactly knew whether there would
be a real meal or just a make-believe; it all de-
pended upon Peter's whim. Make-believe was so
real to him that during a meal of it you could see
him getting rounder.

5 - The Mermaids' Lagoon

THE children spent long summer days on a lagoon. Wendy always hoped she would be able to talk to the mermaids there. She saw them combing their hair on a rock; but when they saw her they dived, splashing her with their tails.

Here by the lagoon the pirates left the cake they had cooked so that the boys might eat it and perish. They placed it in one cunning spot after another; but always Wendy snatched it from the hands of her children. In time it became as hard as a stone, and Hook fell over it in the dark.

In a tree overhanging the lagoon the Never bird built its nest. It fell into the water, and still the bird sat on her eggs.

One day when they were sitting on the rock Wendy noticed that the sun had gone in and it was cold. The lagoon seemed frightening. With a warning cry Peter woke the boys. 'Pirates!' he cried, and gave the order, 'Dive!'

There was a gleam of legs, and instantly the

lagoon seemed deserted. But a boat drew near the rock. It was the pirate dinghy, with three figures in her: Smee and Starkey, and the third, a captive – no other than Tiger Lily. Her hands and ankles were tied, and she knew what was to be her fate. She was to be left on the rock to perish. But she was the daughter of a chief and very brave.

In the gloom the two pirates did not see the rock till they crashed into it.

'Luff, you lubber,' cried Smee's Irish voice. 'Here's the rock. Now then, hoist the redskin on to it, and leave her there to drown.'

It was the work of a moment to land the beautiful girl on the rock. She was too proud to resist.

Quite near the rock, but out of sight, two heads were bobbing up and down – Peter's and Wendy's There was almost nothing Peter could not do, and he now imitated the voice of Hook. 'Ahoy, there, you lubbers,' he called.

'The captain,' said the pirates, staring at each other in surprise. 'He must be swimming out to us,' Starkey said, when they had looked for him in vain.

'We are putting the redskin on the rock,' Smee called out.

'Cut her bonds and let her go,' came the astonishing answer. 'At once, d'ye hear,' cried Peter, in Hook's voice, 'or I'll plunge my hook in you.'

'Better do what the captain orders,' said Starkey.

'Aye, aye,' Smee said, and he cut Tiger Lily's cords. At once like an eel she slid into the water.

Then 'Boat ahoy!' rang over the lagoon in Hook's voice, and this time it was not Peter who had spoken.

'Boat ahoy!' again came the cry. Now Wendy understood. The real Hook was also in the water. He was swimming to the boat. In the light of the lantern Wendy saw his hook grip the boat's side. Peter signed to her to listen.

The two pirates were very curious to know what had brought their captain to them.

'The game's up,' he cried. 'Those boys have found a mother.'

'Captain,' said Smee, 'could we not kidnap these boys' mother and make her our mother?'

'It is a princely scheme,' cried Hook. 'The boys we will make walk the plank, and Wendy shall be our mother. Do you agree, my bullies?'

Starkey and Smee agreed. By this time they were on the rock. Suddenly Hook remembered Tiger Lily. 'Where is the redskin?' he demanded abruptly.

'All right, captain,' said Smee. 'We let her go.'

'You called over the water to us to let her go,' said Starkey.

Hook's face had gone black with rage, but he saw that they believed their words, and he was startled. 'Lads,' he said, shaking a little, 'I gave no such order.'

Hook raised his voice. 'Spirit that haunts this dark lagoon tonight,' he cried, 'dost hear me?'

Peter immediately answered in Hook's voice, 'Odds, bobs, hammers and tongs, I hear you.'

'Who are you, stranger, speak?' Hook demanded.

'I am James Hook,' replied the voice, 'captain of the *Jolly Roger*.'

'You are not,' Hook cried hoarsely.

'Brimstone and gall,' the voice retorted, 'say that again, and I'll cast anchor in you.'

'Do you give it up?' crowed Peter.

'Yes, yes,' the pirates answered eagerly.

'Well, then,' he cried, 'I am Peter Pan.'

In a moment Hook was himself again. 'Now we have him,' he shouted. 'Into the water, Smee. Starkey, mind the boat. Take him dead or alive.'

He leaped as he spoke, and simultaneously came the gay voice of Peter: 'Are you ready, boys?'

'Aye, aye,' from various parts of the lagoon.

'Then lam into the pirates.'

The fight was short and sharp. First to draw blood was John, who gallantly climbed into the boat and held Starkey. There was a fierce struggle, in which the cutlass was torn from the pirate's grasp. He wriggled overboard and John leapt after him. The dinghy drifted away.

Here and there a head bobbed up in the water, and there was a flash of steel, followed by a cry or a whoop. In the confusion some struck at their own side.

Strangely it was not in the water that the pirate captain and Peter Pan met. Hook rose to the rock to breathe, and at the same moment Peter scaled it on the opposite side. The rock was slippery as a ball. Each feeling for a grip felt the other's arm: in surprise they raised their heads; their faces were almost touching; so they met.

Quick as thought Peter snatched a knife from Hook's belt and was about to drive it home, when he saw that he was higher up the rock than his foe.

It would not have been fighting fair. He gave the pirate a hand to help him up.

It was then that Hook bit him. Not the pain of this but its unfairness was what dazed Peter. It made him quite helpless. Twice the iron hand clawed him.

A few minutes afterwards the other boys saw Hook in the water striking wildly for the ship, with fear on his face and the crocodile in dogged pursuit of him.

They found the dinghy and went home in it, shouting, 'Peter, Wendy,' as they went, but no answer came.

There came cold silence over the lagoon, and then a feeble cry, 'Help, help!'

Two small figures were beating against the rock. With a last effort Peter pulled Wendy up the rock and then lay down beside her. The water was rising. He knew that they would soon be drowned, but he had to tell her the truth.

'We are on the rock, Wendy,' he said, 'but it is growing smaller. Soon the water will be over it.'

He told her that Hook had wounded him so that he could neither fly nor swim, but that she must try to get back to the boys without him. Then something brushed against Peter. It was the tail of a kite, which Michael had made some days before. Next moment Peter was pulling the kite towards him.

'It lifted Michael off the ground,' he cried. 'Why should it not carry you?'

Already he had tied the tail round her. She refused to go without him; but with a 'Goodbye, Wendy,' he pushed her from the rock; and in a few minutes she was borne out of his sight.

Steadily the waters rose till they were nibbling at his feet. And now he saw the Never bird making desperate efforts to reach him on her nest. She had come to save him, to give him her nest, though there were eggs in it.

By one last mighty effort the bird propelled the nest against the rock. Then up she flew—deserting her eggs, so as to make her meaning clear. Peter clutched the nest and waved his thanks to the bird as she fluttered overhead.

There was a stave on the rock, driven into it by some buccaneers of long ago to mark the site of buried treasure. The stave was still there, and on it Starkey had hung his hat, a deep tarpaulin, watertight, with a broad brim. Peter put the eggs in this hat and set it on the water.

Then he got into the nest, reared the stave in it as a mast, and hung up his shirt for a sail. At the same moment the bird fluttered down upon the hat and once more sat snugly on her eggs.

Great were the rejoicings when Peter reached the home under the ground. He got there almost as soon as Wendy, who had been carried by the kite.

6 - The Happy Home

PETER had saved Tiger Lily from a dreadful fate, and now there was nothing she and her braves would not do for him. All night the redskins sat above, keeping watch over the home under the ground. Even by day they hung about, smoking the pipe of peace.

One evening, the redskins were at their posts, while, below, the children were having their evening meal; all except Peter, who had gone out to get the time. The way you got the time was to find the crocodile, and then stay near him till the clock struck.

This meal happened to be a make-believe tea, and they sat round the board, guzzling in their greed. The noise was deafening.

When they had finished Wendy told them to clear away. She sat down to her work-basket: a heavy load of stockings, and every knee with a hole in it as usual.

When Peter came back, the gay boys dragged him from his tree. He had brought nuts for them as well as the correct time for Wendy.

Later the boys all got into bed for Wendy's story, the story they loved best, the story Peter hated.

'Listen, then,' said Wendy, settling down with Michael at her feet and seven boys in the bed. 'There was once a gentleman. His name was Mr Darling, and his wife was Mrs Darling. They had three children.

'Now these three children,' went on Wendy, 'had a faithful nurse called Nana. But Mr Darling was angry with her and chained her up in the yard; and so all the children flew away. You see, they knew that their mother would always leave the window open for them to fly back by; so they stayed away for years and had a lovely time.'

'Did they ever go back?' asked the boys.

Yes, Wendy told them. When they wanted to go back they found the window open for them, and they flew in.

When Wendy finished, Peter uttered a groan.

'Wendy, you are wrong about mothers,' he said.

'Long ago I thought like you that my mother would always keep the window open for me. So I stayed away for moons and moons, and then flew back. But the window was barred, for mother had forgotten all about me, and there was another little boy sleeping in my bed.'

'Are you sure mothers are like that?' they asked, scared.

'Yes,' said Peter.

So this was the truth about mothers. The toads!

'Wendy, let us go home,' cried John and Michael; and she clutched them and said, 'Yes.'

'Not tonight?' asked the lost boys.

'At once,' Wendy replied resolutely.

Peter pretended that he did not mind her going, but of course he cared very much.

He went up his tree to talk to the redskins, and when he came down again he told Wendy that they would guide her through the woods.

'Then,' he continued, 'Tinker Bell will take you across the sea. Wake her, Nibs.'

Nibs had to knock twice before he got an answer.

'You are to get up,'he called,'and take Wendy on a journey.'

Of course Tink was delighted to hear that Wendy was going; but she did not want to be her guide, and she said so rudely. Peter spoke to her sternly.

In the meantime the boys were gazing rather forlornly at Wendy, now equipped with John and Michael for the journey.

'Dear ones,' said Wendy, 'if you will all come with me I feel almost sure I can get my father and mother to adopt you.'

The boys jumped with joy. Immediately they rushed to get their things.

'Get *your* things, Peter,' Wendy cried.

'No,' he answered, pretending indifference; 'I am not going with you, Wendy.'

To show that he did not care, he skipped up and

down the room, playing gaily on his pipes. She had to run about after him.

'To find your mother,' she coaxed.

'No, no,' he told Wendy. 'Perhaps she would say I was old, and I just want always to be a little boy and to have fun.'

And so the others had to be told. Peter not coming! They gazed blankly at him, their sticks over their backs, and on each stick a bundle.

'If you find your mothers,' Peter said darkly, 'I hope you will like them. Now then, no fuss, no blubbering. Goodbye, Wendy,' and he held out his hand cheerily.

'Are you ready, Tinker Bell?' he called out. 'Then lead the way.'

Tink darted up the nearest tree; but no one followed her, for it was at this moment that the pirates made their dreadful attack upon the redskins. Above, the air was rent with shrieks and the clash of steel. Below, there was dead silence. Wendy fell on her knees. Peter seized his sword.

7 - The Children are Carried Off

THE pirate attack had been a complete surprise. The redskins, with their blankets folded around them, had been squatting above the children's home, awaiting the morning when they could attack the pirates. Instead, they were found by the treacherous Hook.

Around the brave Tiger Lily were a dozen of her stoutest warriors, and they suddenly saw the pirates bearing down upon them. They seized their weapons, and the air was torn with the war-cry; but it was too late.

Thus perished many of the flower of the Piccaninny tribe. But Tiger Lily and a small remnant of the tribe escaped.

The night's work was not yet over for the pirates. It was Pan Hook wanted, Pan and Wendy and their band, but chiefly Pan.

The question now was how the pirates were to get down the trees to reach the boys in their underground home. Hook ran his greedy eyes over them, searching for the thinnest ones. They wriggled uncomfortably, for they knew that he would not scruple to ram them down with poles.

In the meantime, what of the boys? The pandemonium above had ceased, but they did not know which side had won.

The pirates, listening avidly at the mouths of the trees, heard the question put by every boy, and, alas, they also heard Peter's answer.

'If the redskins have won,' he said, 'they will beat the tom-tom. It is always their sign of victory.'

Now Smee had found the tom-tom, and was at that moment sitting on it. He beat it twice.

'The tom-tom,' the pirates heard Peter cry; 'an Indian victory!'

The children answered with a cheer. Almost immediately they repeated their goodbyes to Peter. The pirates smirked at each other, and rubbed their hands.

Rapidly Hook gave his orders: one man to each tree, and the others to arrange themselves in a line two yards apart.

The first to emerge from his tree was Curly. He rose out of it into the arms of Cecco, who flung him to Smee, and so he was tossed from one to another till he fell at the feet of Captain Hook. All the boys were plucked from their trees in this ruthless manner; and several of them were in the air at a time.

Wendy came last. With ironical politeness Hook raised his hat to her, and, offering her his arm, escorted her to the spot where the others were being gagged.

The children were tied to prevent their flying away, doubled up with their knees close to their ears; and for the trussing of them the black pirate had cut a rope into nine equal pieces. All went well until Slightly's turn came. Every time they tried to pack the unhappy lad tight in one part he bulged out in another.

Hook realized Slightly's secret, which was this: that he was so blown out that any tree big enough for him would also be big enough for a man. Poor Slightly, madly addicted to the drinking of water when he was hot, had swelled so much that he had, unknown to the others, whittled the inside of his tree to make it big enough for him.

This Hook guessed, but he said nothing of the dark design in his mind. He merely signed that the captives were to be taken to the ship, and that he would be alone.

The children were flung into Wendy's house, four stout pirates raised it on their shoulders, the others fell in behind, and singing the hateful pirate chorus the strange procession set off through the wood.

As the little house disappeared in the forest, a brave though tiny jet of smoke issued from its chimney as if defying Hook.

The first thing Hook did on finding himself alone was to tiptoe to Slightly's tree. Intently he listened for any sound, but all was silent. Was Peter Pan asleep, or did he stand waiting at the foot of the tree, dagger in hand?

Hook stepped into the tree. He arrived at the foot of the shaft, and stood still again. As his eyes became accustomed to the dim light he saw the great bed. On the bed lay Peter fast asleep.

Unaware of the tragedy above, Peter had continued after the children left to play gaily on his pipes to prove to himself that he did not care. Then he decided not to take his medicine, so as to grieve Wendy who had left it ready for him. Then he lay down on the bed and fell asleep in the middle of it.

Thus defenceless, Hook found him.

Though a light from the lamp shone dimly on the bed Hook stood in darkness. But what was that? The red in his eye had caught sight of Peter's medicine standing on a ledge.

Hook always carried about his person a dreadful drug – a yellow liquid poison. Five drops of this he now added to Peter's cup. His hand shook. Then he cast one long gloating look upon his victim, and turning, wormed his way with difficulty up the tree. He looked the very spirit of evil, as he stole away through the forest.

Peter slept on. It must have been not less than ten o'clock by the crocodile when he suddenly sat up in his bed, wakened by a soft cautious tapping on the door of his tree.

A lovely bell-like voice called: 'Let me in, Peter.' It was Tink. She flew in excitedly, her face flushed and her dress stained with mud.

'What is it?' asked Peter; and in one long ungrammatical sentence she told of the capture of Wendy and the boys.

Peter's heart bobbed up and down as he listened. Wendy bound, and on the pirate ship!

'I'll rescue her,' he cried, leaping at his weapons. As he leapt he thought of something he could do to please her. He could take his medicine. His hand closed on the fatal draught.

'No!' shrieked Tinker Bell, who had heard Hook muttering to himself as he sped through the forest.

'Why not?'

'Hook has poisoned it.'

'Don't be silly,' said Peter. 'How could Hook have got down here?'

Alas, Tinker Bell could not explain this, for even she did not know the dark secret of Slightly's tree. But Hook's words had left no room for doubt. The cup was poisoned.

Peter raised the cup. With one of her lightning movements Tink got between his lips and the draught, and drained it to the dregs.

Already she was reeling in the air. 'It was poisoned, Peter,' she told him softly; 'and now I am going to be dead. I drank it to save you.'

Her wings would scarcely carry her now, and, tottering to her chamber, she lay down on the bed. Every moment her light was growing fainter, and Peter knew that if it went out she would be no more.

Her voice was so low that at first he could not make out what she said. Then he made it out. She was saying that she thought she could get well again if children believed in fairies.

Peter flung out his arms. He addressed all children who might be dreaming of the Neverland.

'Do you believe?' he cried. 'If you believe, clap your hands. Don't let Tink die.'

Many clapped. Some didn't. A few little beasts hissed.

Already Tink was saved. First her voice grew

strong. Then she was flashing through the room more merry and impudent than ever.

'And now to rescue Wendy.' The moon was riding in a cloudy sky when Peter rose from his tree, begirt with weapons, to set out upon his perilous quest. It was not a night he would have chosen. A slight fall of snow had obliterated all footmarks, and a deadly silence pervaded the island.

The crocodile passed him, but not another living thing. He swore this terrible oath: 'Hook or me this time.'

8 - The Pirate Ship

ONE green light marked where the brig, the *Jolly Roger*, lay, low in the water. The night was dark. There was little sound save the whir of the ship's sewing machine at which Smee sat.

Hook trod the deck in thought. It was his hour of triumph. Peter had been removed for ever from his path, and all the other boys were on the brig, about to walk the plank.

But Hook was gloomy. For long he muttered to himself, staring at Smee, who was hemming placidly. There was not a child on board the brig that night who did not already love Smee. He had said horrid things to them and hit them with the palm of his hand, because he was too kind to hit with his fist; but they had only clung to him the more. Michael had tried on his spectacles.

'Quiet, you scugs,' Hook cried to some of the pirates who had broken into a dance, 'or I'll cast anchor in you with my hook. Are all the children chained, so they cannot fly away?'

'Aye, aye.'

'Then hoist them up on deck.'

The wretched prisoners were dragged from the hold, all except Wendy, and ranged in line in front of him. The boys went white when they saw Jukes and Cecco preparing the fatal plank. But they tried to look brave when Wendy was brought up.

'So, my beauty,' said Hook, as if he spoke in syrup, 'you are to see your children walk the plank.'

It was Smee who tied her to the mast. 'See here, honey,' he whispered, 'I'll save you if you promise to be my mother.'

But not even for Smee would she make such a promise.

The eyes of all the boys were on the plank: that last little walk they were about to take. They could only stare and shiver.

Hook smiled on them with his teeth closed, and

took a step towards Wendy. He meant to turn her face so that she should see the boys walking the plank one by one. But he never reached her. He heard something instead.

It was the terrible tick-tick of the crocodile. They all heard it – pirates, boys, Wendy, and immediately every head was blown in one direction—towards Hook.

It was frightful to see the change that came over him. It was as if he had been clipped at every joint.

The sound came steadily nearer. Hook crawled on his knees along the deck as far from it as he could go. The pirates made way for him.

'Hide me,' he cried hoarsely. They gathered round him, all eyes averted from the thing that was coming aboard.

The boys rushed to the ship's side to see the crocodile climbing in. Then they got the strangest surprise of this Night of Nights; for it was no crocodile that was coming to their aid. It was Peter – ticking.

When last we saw Peter he was stealing across the island, his dagger at the ready. He had seen the crocodile pass by without noticing anything peculiar about it, but by and by he remembered that it had not been ticking. The clock had run down.

Peter at once decided to tick, so that wild beasts

should believe he was the crocodile and let him pass unmolested. He ticked superbly, but with one unforeseen result. The crocodile heard the sound and it followed him.

Peter reached the shore without mishap, and went straight on into the water. As he swam he had but one thought: 'Hook or me this time!' He had ticked so long that he now went on ticking without knowing that he was doing it.

He thought he had scaled the side of the brig as noiseless as a mouse; and he was amazed to see the pirates cowering from him, with Hook in their midst as abject as if he had heard the crocodile.

The crocodile! No sooner did Peter remember it than he heard the ticking. At first he thought the sound did come from the crocodile, and he looked behind him swiftly. Then he realized that he was doing it himself. 'How clever of me,' he thought at once, and signed to the boys not to burst into applause.

Peter, every inch of him on tiptoe, vanished into the cabin.

'It's gone, captain,' Smee said, wiping his spectacles. 'All's still again.'

Slowly Hook let his head emerge from his ruff. There was not a sound, and he drew himself up firmly to his full height.

'Then here's to Johnny Plank,' he cried brazenly. He broke into the villainous ditty:

> *'Yo ho, yo ho, the frisky plank,*
> *You walks along it so,*
> *Till it goes down and you goes down*
> *To Davy Jones below!'*

'Fetch the cat-o'-nine-tails, Jukes,' said Hook; 'it's in the cabin.'

The cabin! Peter was in the cabin! The children gazed at each other.

'Aye, aye,' said Jukes blithely, and he strode into the cabin. They followed him with their eyes.

There was a dreadful screech from the cabin. It wailed through the ship, and died away. Then was heard a crowing sound which was well understood by the boys, but to the pirates was almost more eerie than the screech.

'What was that?' cried Hook.

Cecco hesitated for a moment, and then swung into the cabin. He tottered out, haggard.

'What's the matter with Bill Jukes, you dog?'

'The matter wi' him is he's dead, stabbed,' replied Cecco in a hollow voice. 'The cabin's as black as a pit, but there is something terrible in there: the thing you heard crowing.'

Hook rallied his men with a gesture. ''Sdeath and

odds fish,' he thundered, 'who is to bring me that doodle-doo? I think I heard you volunteer, Starkey?'

'No, by thunder!' Starkey cried. 'I'll swing before I go in there.'

'Is it mutiny?' asked Hook. 'Starkey's ring-leader.'

'Captain, mercy,' Starkey whimpered.

'Shake hands, Starkey,' said Hook, proffering his claw.

Starkey looked round for help, but all deserted him. With a despairing scream the pirate leapt upon Long Tom and precipitated himself into the sea.

'And now,' Hook asked courteously, 'did any other

gentleman say mutiny?' Seizing a lantern and raising his claw with a menacing gesture, 'I'll bring out that doodle-doo myself,' Hook said, and sped into the cabin.

He came staggering out, without his lantern.

'Something blew out the light,' he said.

The mutinous sounds again broke forth. One after another the pirates took up the cry, 'The ship's doomed.' At this the children could not resist raising a cheer. Hook had well-nigh forgotten his prisoners, but now his face lit up again.

'Lads,' he cried to his crew, 'here's a notion. Open the cabin door and drive them in. Let them fight the doodle-doo. If they kill him, we're so much the better; if he kills them, we're none the worse.'

The boys, pretending to struggle, were pushed into the cabin and the door was closed on them.

'Now, listen,' cried Hook, and all listened. But not one pirate dared to face the door.

In the cabin Peter had found the thing for which he had gone in search: the key that would free the children of the manacles which chained them together. And now they all stole forth, armed with such weapons as they could find.

First signing to the boys to hide, Peter cut Wendy's bonds. He whispered to her to conceal herself with the others, and himself took her place by the mast,

73

her cloak around him. Then he took a great breath and crowed.

The pirates were panic-stricken.

Hook told them it was unlucky to have a girl on a pirate ship, and they must fling Wendy overboard. The men made a rush at the figure in the cloak.

'None can save you now, missy,' Mullins hissed.

'There's one,' replied the figure.

'Who's that?'

'Peter Pan the avenger!' came the terrible answer; and as he spoke Peter flung off his cloak.

'Down, boys, and at them,' Peter's voice rang out; and in another moment the clash of arms was resounding through the ship.

Again and again the boys closed upon Hook, and again and again he hewed a clear space. He had lifted up one boy with his hook, and was using him as a buckler, when another sprang into the fray.

'Put up your swords, boys,' cried the newcomer; 'this man is mine.'

Then suddenly Hook found himself face to face with Peter. The others formed a ring round them.

For long the two enemies looked at one another. Then they fell to. Peter was a superb swordsman, but he was too small to drive his sword home. Hook forced him back. Peter, lunging fiercely, pierced him in the ribs. At sight of his own blood, whose peculiar colour was offensive to him, the sword fell from Hook's hand, and he was at Peter's mercy.

'Now!' cried all the boys; but with a magnificent gesture Peter invited him to pick up his sword.

Hook was fighting now without hope. Seeing Peter slowly advancing upon him with dagger poised, he sprang upon the bulwarks to cast himself into the sea—and crocodile was waiting for him.

Thus perished James Hook.

Fifteen pirates paid the penalty for their crimes that night; but two reached the shore: Starkey to be captured by the redskins, who made him nurse for all their papooses, a melancholy come-down for a pirate; and Smee, who henceforth wandered about the world in his spectacles.

9 - The Return Home

THE children slept in the pirates' bunks that night.

By two bells next morning they were all stirring their stumps, for there was a big sea running. They all donned pirate clothes cut off at the knee, and tumbled up on deck.

It need not be said who was the captain. Peter had already lashed himself to the wheel. A few sharp orders were given, and they turned the ship round, and nosed her for the mainland.

Captain Pan calculated that if this weather lasted they should strike the Azores about the 21st of June, after which it would save time to fly.

Wendy and John and Michael were looking forward to their mother's surprise when they got back to Number 14. Meanwhile in the night-nursery the only change to be seen was that between nine and six Nana's kennel was no longer there. When the children flew away, Mr Darling felt that all the blame was his for having chained Nana up so that she could not take care of them properly. And he went down on all fours and crawled into the kennel.

In his remorse he said that he would never leave the kennel until his children came back. There never was a more humble man than the once proud George Darling. Every morning the kennel was carried with him in it to a cab, which took him to his office; and he returned home in the same way at six.

On this eventful Thursday Mrs Darling was in the night-nursery, a very sad-eyed woman. The children were within two miles of the window now, and flying strong – but of course she did not know it. Mr Darling was as usual in the kennel.

'Won't you play me to sleep,' he asked, 'on the nursery piano?' and as she was crossing to the day-nursery, he added thoughtlessly, 'And shut that window. I feel a draught.'

'Oh George, never ask me to do that. The window must always be left open for them, always, always.'

She went into the nursery and played, and soon he was asleep; and while he slept, Wendy and John and Michael flew into the room. They alighted on the floor.

It was then that Mrs Darling began playing again. 'It's mother!' cried Wendy, peeping. 'Let us all slip into our beds, and be there when she comes in, just as if we had never been away.'

And so when Mrs Darling went back to the night-nursery to see if her husband was asleep, all the beds were occupied. When she saw the children she could not believe at first that they were real. Then she stretched out her arms. Wendy and John and Michael slipped out of bed and ran to her.

'George, George,' she cried when she could speak. Mr Darling woke to share her bliss, and Nana came rushing in. There could not have been a lovelier sight; but there was none to see it except a strange boy who was staring in at the window.

The other boys were waiting below to give Wendy time to explain about them; and when they had counted five hundred they went up: by the stairs, because they thought this would make a better impression. They stood in a row in front of Mrs Darling, with their hats off, and wishing they were not wearing their pirate clothes. They said nothing, but their eyes asked her to have them.

Of course Mrs Darling said at once that she would have them; but they saw that Mr Darling considered six a rather large number. The first Twin was the proud one, and he asked, flushing, 'Do you think we should be too much of a handful, sir? Because if so we can go away.'

'We could lie doubled up,' said Nibs.

'I always cut their hair myself,' said Wendy.

Mr Darling said he would find space for them all in the drawing-room.

'We'll fit in, sir,' they assured him.

As for Peter, he saw Wendy once again before he flew away. He did not exactly come to the window,

but he brushed against it in passing, so that she could open it if she liked and call to him. That was what she did.

'Hallo, Wendy, goodbye,' he said.

'Oh dear, are you going away?'

'Yes.'

Mrs Darling came to the window, for at present she was keeping a sharp eye on Wendy.

'But where are you going to live?' she asked Peter.

'With Tink in the house we built for Wendy. The fairies are to put it high up among the tree tops where they sleep at nights. I shall have such fun,' said Peter, with one eye on Wendy.

'It will be rather lonely in the evening,' she said, 'sitting by the fire.'

'Well, come with me to the little house,' said Peter.

'May I, mummy?' asked Wendy.

'Certainly not. I have got you home again, and I mean to keep you.'

'Oh, all right,' Peter said, as if he had asked her from politeness merely; but Mrs Darling saw his mouth twitch, and she made this handsome offer: to let Wendy go to him for a week every year to do his spring-cleaning.

'You won't forget me, Peter, will you, before spring-cleaning time comes?' asked Wendy.

Of course Peter promised; and then he flew away.